S0-ABC-249

SHARK ATTACK ALMANAC

BY MARY BATTEN
ILLUSTRATED BY CAROL LYON

KidBacks™

RANDOM HOUSE 🏠 NEW YORK

ACKNOWLEDGMENTS

I am most grateful to the following for generously sharing their work, ideas, and experiences with me: Stephen Arrington, author of *High on Adventure;* George H. Balazs, National Marine Fisheries Service, Honolulu Laboratory; George H. Burgess, Director, International Shark Attack File, American Elasmobranch Society; Ralph Collier; Jean-Michel Cousteau, Jean-Michel Cousteau Productions; Mike deGruy, producer, The Film Crew, Inc.; Rodney Fox; Christopher Lowe, Hawaii Institute of Marine Biology; Michael Martinez; John Naughton, Pacific Islands Environmental Coordinator, National Fisheries Service; Dr. Don Nelson, California State University, Long Beach; Yehuda Goldman, Executive Director of Hydrosphere, Pacific Palisades, California; Dr. Jeff Seigel, Los Angeles County Museum of Natural History; and Rocky Strong, University of California, Santa Barbara.

Copyright © 1997 by RGA Publishing Group, Inc.

All rights reserved under International and Pan-American Copyright Conventions. Published in the United States by Random House, Inc., New York, and simultaneously in Canada by Random House of Canada Limited, Toronto.

Library of Congress Cataloging-in-Publication Data
Batten, Mary.
    Shark attack almanac / by Mary Batten ; illustrated by Carol Lyon.
       p. cm. — (KidBacks)
    Summary: Provides information about the physical characteristics and behavior of various species of sharks and accounts of the not-so-common attacks of sharks on humans.
    ISBN 0-679-87769-X (pbk.)
    1. Shark attacks—Juvenile literature. 2. Sharks—Juvenile literature.
[1. Sharks. 2. Shark attacks.] I. Lyon, Carol, 1963- ill. II. Title. III. Series.
QL638.93.B38 1997
597'.31—dc20   96-42324
         http://www.randomhouse.com/

Printed in the United States of America

10 9 8 7 6 5 4 3 2 1

KIDBACKS ™ is a trademark of Random House, Inc.

CONTENTS

INTRODUCTION

W E CAN ALL IMAGINE IT: You are swimming alone in the ocean when, suddenly, you are pulled below the surface. You thrash about. What's happening? The water turns red with blood. *Your* blood. You surface and scream—your body is in the grip of razor-sharp teeth lining a gargantuan jaw. It hits you. *You're being eaten by a shark!*

If you are like most people, you are terrified of sharks. You may never have even seen a real shark, but you can *feel* the fear. Even people who don't swim or go into the water fear sharks. The reason is simple: Sharks can eat us alive. In the sea, *they* are the masters. We humans are helpless aliens, unable to run and hide as we can on land.

Shark attacks make headlines. *Big* headlines. Because of all this media attention, you might think shark attacks are quite common. They aren't. Throughout the entire world, there are 70 to 100 shark attacks each year, resulting in five to ten deaths. When you consider there are 5.6 billion people living on the planet, this makes the risk of death by shark attack about one in a billion.

Fear of shark attack is far out of proportion to the facts. On average, 40 to 50 people die of snakebites and bee stings, and about 100 people are killed by lightning, each year in the United States alone. You are far more likely to die in a car accident on your way to the beach than from an attack by a shark you may encounter there in the water.

In this book, you'll learn how to separate Hollywood's fictional sharks from the real animals that swim in the world's oceans. You'll read accounts of some of the most well-documented shark attacks. You'll also find stories of personal encounters with sharks by some of the world's most experienced divers. So dive into the mysterious underwater world and get the inside track on why sharks attack!

THE MASTER PREDATOR

"When a shark comes up to my face and looks into my eyes, I feel that I'm with one of the most magnificent creatures in the world."

Dr. Eugenie Clark, shark scientist

SHARKS INSPIRE RESPECT. No doubt about it. They are the most perfect predators that have ever lived. Everything about the shark—its body shape, teeth, eyesight, hearing, sense of smell, and special electrical sensors—has evolved for hunting, killing, and eating prey with awesome efficiency.

"Sharks have better sensory abilities than almost anything else in the sea," says George Burgess, director of the International Shark Attack File (ISAF) at the Florida Museum of Natural History, University of Florida, Gainesville, Florida.

Scientists call sharks "keystone" or "apex" predators, because they are at the top of the ocean's food chain. This means that they have few predators and can eat whatever they want. White sharks, for example, like to eat seals, dolphins, and sea lions, which in turn feed on smaller fishes, and so on down the food chain. Sharks keep populations of fishes in balance and clean the oceans of weak, dead, and dying animals. Almost all animals—with the exception of three or four species of sharks—are both hunters and hunted. The smallest animals of the sea, plankton, form the base of the food chain and are preyed upon by more animals than anything else in the sea.

Sharks have had a lot of time to develop their hunting abilities: some 400 million years, approximately. Long before dinosaurs ruled the land, the first sharks evolved. But those early sharks are extinct. The ancestors of most sharks found in the oceans today appeared later, during the Jurassic Period, 210 to 144 million years ago, when dinosaurs flourished.

What Makes a Shark a Shark?

While more than 350 different species of sharks inhabit the world's oceans, there are certain basic features that all sharks share.

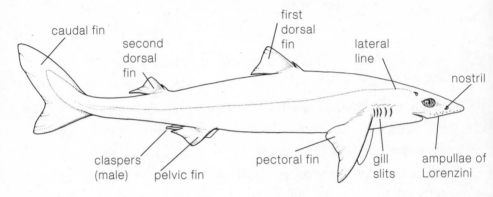

The spiny dogfish shark—the shark most commonly studied by research scientists

BONELESS BODIES

Make no bones about it, the shark is a very special kind of fish. In fact, it has *no bones* in its body. Unlike most other fishes, whose skeletons are made of bone, sharks and their relatives—the strange-looking rays and sawfishes—have skeletons that are made of cartilage. This is why they are called cartilaginous (car-ti-LADGE-uh-nus) fishes, or elasmobranchs (ih-LAS-mo-branks).

Cartilage is a strong, rubbery tissue that is also called gristle. You can feel the difference between bone and cartilage. Touch your ear. See how easily it bends? It is made of cartilage. Now touch the side of your jaw. It feels very hard because it is made of bone, like the rest of the human skeleton.

6

Cartilage is more flexible and lighter than bone. This gives sharks great freedom of movement. Their torpedo-like bodies are stream-lined for fast, efficient movement through the water. How fast can sharks swim? Since they don't come with built-in speedometers, it's impossible to get a precise measurement; but the super-streamlined mako shark has been observed jumping approximately 18 feet out of the water. To make such a leap, it would have to be swimming about 22 miles per hour. Sharks do not swim that fast all the time, how-ever. They usually just turn on the speed when pursuing and attack-ing prey.

FINS

All sharks have fins—the balancing and steering organs extending from their bodies. Most sharks have a total of eight fins. The largest of the two dorsal (back) fins is located near the middle of the shark's back. This is the fin you see cutting through the water when a shark is swimming near the surface. The other dorsal fin, which is much smaller, is closer to the tail.

GILLS

If you were a shark, you would breathe through gills—organs that sharks and other fishes use to get oxygen from water—rather than using your lungs. Most sharks have five gill slits on each side of the body, near the pec-toral (chest) fins, but a few species have six or seven. Just as we breathe oxygen in the air, sharks and other fishes breathe oxygen dissolved in water. The shark breathes in

gill slits

carbon dioxide

oxygen-carrying water

gills

shark's breathing system

by opening its mouth, allowing oxygen-carrying water to pass over the gills. The oxygen then passes through the thin gill membranes into the shark's bloodstream and travels throughout its body. Just as we exhale carbon dioxide through our nose, the shark breathes out this waste product through its gill slits.

NOSE

Because of its amazing sense of smell, the shark has a reputation as a "swimming nose." The nostrils are on the underside of the snout, in front of the mouth. As the shark swims along, it constantly "sniffs" the water to catch the odor of prey.

This is how the shark's nose works: When the shark takes in water through its mouth to circulate oxygen to its gills, some water flows into the nostrils. Each nostril opens into a nasal sac filled with sensory cells that help the shark detect even the faintest odor.

If a shark gets a whiff of possible prey, it follows the scent like a hunting dog, moving relentlessly in the direction of the animal giving off the odor. Sharks can pick up a scent that is more than a *mile* (2 kilometers) away.

Fish blood is guaranteed to get a shark's attention. Sharks are strongly attracted to the slightest amount of fish blood and other body fluids or chemicals given off by wounded or frightened fish. No big surprise here: Fish are most sharks' normal prey. Scientists have found that lemon sharks can detect one part of tuna juice mixed with 25 million parts of seawater!

Sharks that have been deprived of food are even more sensitive to odor. In laboratory experiments, the late marine biologist Albert Tester, who was professor of zoology at the University of Hawaii, learned that starving blacktip sharks could detect one part of concentrated grouper flesh in 10 *billion* parts of seawater.

Sharks are also attracted to the scent of garbage.

8

EYES

Sharks can see objects as far away as 50 feet (15 meters), but they probably cannot see distinct shapes and colors as well as we can. They are very sensitive to movement and to pale or contrasting colors. This ability is particularly important in the often-murky sea, where the only visual cue to locating prey might be a flash of silver skin or a sudden movement.

Sharks have a mirrorlike structure in their eyes called the tapetum lucidum (tuh-PEE-tum loo-SEE-dum), which

---

SHARK ATTACK FACT

MYTH: One microscopic drop of human blood in the water can trigger a shark attack.

FACT: There is no evidence to support this belief. Shark scientist Dr. H. David Baldridge studied 1,165 shark attacks, occurring from 1941 through 1968, from the International Shark Attack File and found only 19 cases in which the victims were bleeding in the water before the attack. He also found many instances in which the shark struck the victim once and left without any further attack—even though the victim was bleeding profusely from huge wounds. This is not to say that human blood is *never* a turn-on for these unpredictable animals. When some large sharks, such as the tiger shark, are hungry, they will go after anything.

---

reflects light, enabling species that feed at night to see in even the dimmest conditions. For sharks that also feed in daylight, the tapetum has a built-in screen—kind of like sunglasses—that keeps bright light from harming the retina. The retina is the part of the eye that acts like film in a camera, enabling animals to see.

Most sharks have color vision and are especially sensitive to contrasting colors—such as uneven tan lines on people's bodies—which they can see from many feet below the surface of the water. Experiments suggest that the great white shark, which feeds mostly during the day, uses its vision to help identify prey. While all sharks use vision when their prey are close enough to see, some sharks close their eyes while they're feeding.

Some sharks have fixed eyelids that don't move, others have movable eyelids, and a few species have a third eyelid, called a nictitating (NICK-tih-tay-ting) membrane, which completely covers the eye during feeding.

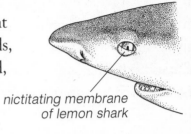

nictitating membrane
of lemon shark

ELECTRICAL SENSORS

No animal on land or in the sea has electrical sensors that can compare with the shark's. All living animals, including humans, give off weak electrical currents called animal electricity. Sharks are more sensitive to these currents than any other animal because of unique sensory organs on their snout. These organs, called the ampullae (am-POOL-ee) of Lorenzini (lor-un-ZEE-nee), enable sharks to find prey by homing in on the prey's electrical fields.

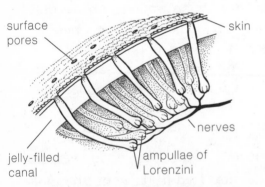

surface pores

skin

nerves

jelly-filled canal

ampullae of Lorenzini

The ampullae of Lorenzini are a series of jelly-filled pores containing sensitive nerve endings. All sharks have these special pores. The ampullae of Lorenzini act like antennas, picking up electrical signals and sending them to the shark's brain.

Experiments have demonstrated that sharks can use their electric sensors to find fish that try to hide by burrowing beneath the sand. Some scientists believe that sharks can sense the earth's magnetic field and use this ability to navigate through the oceans.

VIBRATION SENSORS

If someone moves close to you, you can sometimes sense their vibrations before you see them. Sharks and other fishes also have this ability, but they are much more sensitive than we are. Sharks and all other fishes are "wired" to sense very small vibrations in the water. Extending along the sides of the head and body is a system of fluid-filled canals containing hairlike receptors that enable sharks and other fishes to sense the slightest movement or change in pressure around them up to 100 feet (31 meters) away. These canals are known as the lateral-line system.

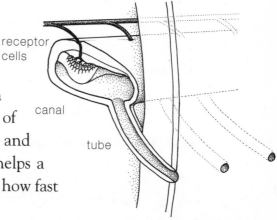

Sharks also detect vibrations with their ears and can hear sounds up to a distance of 1,000 feet (305 meters) and beyond. Its sense of hearing helps a shark to know its position and how fast it is swimming.

detail of lateral-line system

THOSE TEETH!

Life as an apex predator in the ocean's food chain takes its toll on a shark's teeth. They are constantly being broken off by the general wear and tear of ripping and chomping prey. But no worry here. New teeth continue to grow throughout a shark's life—which may last 30 years or more. Each new tooth is a little bit larger than the one it replaces. According to the book *Sharks in Question: The Smithsonian Answer Book* by Victor Springer and Joy Gold, it has been estimated that some individual sharks may shed as many as 30,000 teeth in a lifetime. Imagine the expense of being tooth fairy to a shark!

All sharks have five or more rows of teeth in their jaws, and a few species have as many as eight. You may *see* only one or two rows—the teeth that are in use. The others are folded back in the jaw tissue, ready to rotate into position when needed. An adult tiger shark, for example, may have a new row of teeth rotate into place every seven to ten days. Captive lemon sharks replace teeth every seven to eight days.

Sharks' teeth come in all sizes, shapes, and designs, depending on the largeness of the shark and what it eats. Different species have characteristic teeth. Flesh-eaters like the great white, bull, and tiger sharks have razor-sharp, pointed teeth. Even within one species of shark, differences can be found. Teeth from the upper and lower jaws may or may not look the same; sometimes the teeth in the upper jaw are large and triangular, while smaller, more daggerlike teeth appear in the lower.

FEEDING FRENZY

Snap! Slash! Chomp! Sharks in a feeding frenzy will attack anything that moves, including each other. A frenzy is a highly excited feeding state that is usually triggered by strong odors or sounds that the sharks think are coming from possible food. While sharks spend most of their time slowly cruising through the ocean in peaceful groups or alone, they can become extremely excited by a struggling fish, fish blood, or an abundance of prey, such as groups of seals and sea lions. Any of these conditions can trigger a feeding frenzy. The behavior is quite spectacular, with sharks slashing and biting even as they are dying of wounds themselves. Scientists think that feeding frenzies occur when sharks' brains become so stimulated that they go into sensory overload and lose all inhibitions. Similar behavior occurs among some species of birds and even among humans, as in mob riots.

A shark usually catches its prey with its lower-jaw teeth, then uses the upper-jaw teeth to rip through a section of flesh.

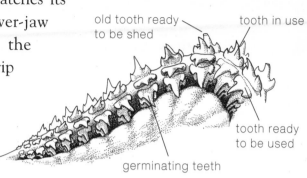

old tooth ready to be shed

tooth in use

tooth ready to be used

germinating teeth

porbeagle shark jaw

Some species of shark, though, have teeth that are not used for chomping, ripping, or tearing. The gigantic whale shark, the largest fish in the sea, and the basking shark, the second-largest fish, have very tiny teeth that play no part in feeding. These large sharks are called filter feeders. They eat plankton—microscopic animals and plants that drift through the sea. The basking shark's mouth is filled with gill rakers, or strainers. It swims with its big mouth wide open and filters as much as 400,000 gallons (1.5 million liters) of water per hour.

closeup of hammerhead shark's skin

SKIN

The shark not only has a toothy mouth, it has toothy skin. Unlike the thin, flaky scales found on other fishes, the shark's body is covered with millions of tiny, hard, toothlike scales called denticles. Each species of shark has its own particular shape and size of denticle. But all shark skin has at least one thing in common— it's rough and abrasive. It's possible to get a severe skin scrape just from bumping into a shark's body.

13

How Sharks Have Babies

For all sharks, fertilization—when a male's sperm penetrate a female's eggs—takes place inside the female's body. When a male mates with a female, he often bites her pectoral fin to hold on to her. The male shark does not have a penis. His reproductive organs are called pelvic claspers, of which he has two. While holding the female with his mouth, he uses his pelvic claspers to deposit sperm into her special sperm-storage chamber, the cloaca (clo-AY-kuh).

After the eggs are fertilized, the female's shell gland secretes a protective case over them. Females have two ovaries, but usually only one produces eggs. The other one shrivels and is never used.

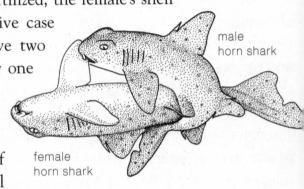

male
horn shark

female
horn shark

About 30 percent of all sharks, including swell sharks, horn sharks, and many cat sharks, lay each of their fertilized eggs in hard, leathery cases on the sandy ocean bottom or in vegetation growing on the bottom. After laying their eggs, the females leave. (There is no such thing as parental care in the shark world.) These egg cases have very distinctive shapes. The Port Jackson shark's and the horn shark's egg cases look like huge screws. The swell shark's egg case has curly tendrils that hold it to underwater vegetation and keep it from being washed ashore.

Inside sharks' egg cases, the shark embryos feed on large egg yolks. When the embryo has eaten all its egg yolk and has no more food, it hatches out of its egg case and swims away to fend for itself.

In another 60 percent of shark species, the fertilized eggs remain inside the mother's *two* uteruses. The embryos hatch inside the mother and are born live into the water. Among sand tiger, mako, and thresher sharks, a cannibalistic drama unfolds inside the mother's body.

The first sand tiger shark embryo to break free of its egglike capsule swims around its mother's uterus, ripping open the hundreds of other egg capsules and eating its unhatched brothers and sisters! This goes on inside each of the female's two uteruses. Although the embryos are only about four inches long, they already have sharp teeth. The cannibalism continues until there are only two survivors, one from each uterus. By the time these two are born, each baby is about 40 inches long, and well prepared for its role as a predator.

In a few species, such as hammerheads, blue sharks, and bull sharks, embryos are not encased in eggs but are connected to the mother's uterus by an umbilical cord, as in mammals. When the females of these species are ready to give birth, they may swim to nurs-

horn shark's egg case

swell shark's egg case

SHARK BYTE!

The great white shark may be humongous in size, but its extinct relative *Carcharodon megalodon* (CAR-kah-ruh-don MEG-uh-low-don) was the largest flesh-eating shark that ever lived. *Carcharodon megalodon* swam the seas between 5 and 25 million years ago, long before the earliest humans appeared. Some of its fossil teeth are six inches long and weigh 12 ounces—the same as a can of soda! Based on the size of its teeth and a jaw reconstructed by shark experts, scientists estimate that *Carcharodon megalodon* grew up to 50 feet in length and weighed up to 20 tons, roughly the weight of two and a half African elephants.

ery areas, where the waters are warm and contain abundant food. Baby sharks are called pups, and they look like tiny adults as they squirm out of the female's body and begin swimming. Females of some species have only a single pup; others may bear as many as a hundred.

In all live births, once a baby is born, the mother swims away. The shark baby is left to survive on its own.

Shark Lover ♥   **JEAN-MICHEL COUSTEAU**

"Sharks are not man-eaters, but some are man-biters," says the famous ocean explorer Jean-Michel Cousteau. "Because they don't have hands to feel things, they feel with their mouth and their teeth. Usually sharks bite and release, because they realize the human (whom they've bitten into) is not what they expected. By then they've usually damaged their victim, and depending on the damage, the injured person can bleed to death."

From 1989 to 1992, Jean-Michel Cousteau, whose father is the pioneering diver and explorer Jacques-Yves Cousteau, led the most ambitious expedition ever undertaken to study great white sharks. It was the longest study of white sharks to date, involving a team of some 40 scientists, divers, cameramen, and sailors from around the world. The expedition was centered around Dangerous Reef, Australia, an area known for its population of great whites.

Although Jean-Michel has been diving for more than 50 years, he has never had a frightening experience with sharks. "If I know there are conditions for a potential shark attack . . . or I'm in an area where sharks normally feed, I get out. You're entering their domain when you get into the water; thus, respect needs to prevail."

ATTACKS

"I looked down, and the picture that remains with me today is the nightmare we all worry about—blood-red water and this great, big head with its mouth wide open, coming up to eat me."

Rodney Fox, shark attack survivor

SHARK ATTACKS ARE EXTREMELY RARE, but when they happen, they make big, blaring headlines.

The first reliably documented shark attack occurred in 1580. Somewhere between India and Portugal, a sailor fell overboard. His friends threw him a rope and were hauling him back to the ship when a shark attacked. According to an eyewitness, "There appeared from below the surface of the sea a *tiburón* [the Spanish word for "shark"]. It rushed at the man and tore him to pieces before our very eyes."

Today, the most reliable information about shark attacks is kept by the International Shark Attack File in Gainesville, Florida, with support from the American Elasmobranch Society. This is a professional organization of scientists who study Elasmobranchii (**ih-las-mo-BRANK-ee**), the group of cartilaginous fishes that includes sharks, skates, and rays. The file was started in 1958 by the U.S. Navy and was originally housed at the Smithsonian Institution in Washington, D.C.

When marine biologists around the world investigate shark attacks, they routinely send reports to the Shark Attack File. From the first known attack in 1580 to the most recent one, as of this writing, in February 1996, there have been 2,764 investigations of shark attacks worldwide. This data reveals that 407 people have been killed in unprovoked attacks.

How Sharks Attack

According to George Burgess, director of the Shark Attack File, there are three major kinds of unprovoked shark attacks: "Hit and Run," "Bump and Bite," and "Sneak."

Hit and Run

In this most common type of attack, the victim seldom sees the shark, which bites once and leaves. It usually occurs right offshore, often to swimmers and surfers. Scientists believe hit and run attacks are cases of mistaken identity that take place in murky or rough water where it's difficult for the shark to see. For example, viewed from below, a person on a surfboard may resemble a seal or a turtle, animals that are favorite foods of great whites and tiger sharks.

Bump and Bite

The next two types of attacks are much less common but result in more serious injuries and fatalities. Divers or swimmers in deeper waters are the usual victims. In the bump and bite, the shark circles and often bumps the victim before the actual attack, which then involves several bites that inflict severe wounds.

Sneak

Sneak attacks occur without any circling or other "warning" by the shark. Sharks that make such attacks are probably feeding or defending themselves against what they think is a threat from the human. Most shark attacks on downed pilots and shipwrecked sailors are probably the bump and bite or sneak types.

Where Shark Attacks Occur

From 1990 to 1995, there were a total of 283 reported shark attacks worldwide. Of those, 203 occurred in six areas—Florida, Brazil, South Africa, Hawaii, California, and Australia—and only 18 were fatal. According to the ISAF, more shark attacks occur in Florida than anyplace else on earth. This is because more people go into the ocean in this area. Brazil has the second largest number of shark attacks, followed by South Africa, Hawaii, California, and Australia. The remaining attacks took place in various other regions, including the island of Réunion in the Indian Ocean, Hong Kong, Japan, and New Zealand.

Straight Facts on Shark Attacks

Most shark attacks have certain things in common:

• More than 90 percent of attacks occur during daylight hours— when more people are in the water.

• Most attacks occur in less than six feet of water, but a few have occurred in less than three feet.

• Sharks tend to attack objects that are bright and shiny, or that have a contrasting and/or reflective appearance.

• Sharks follow ships to feed on discarded food, and they tend to gather along shorelines close to garbage-dumping sites.

• Sharks prefer to bite men. Approximately ten times more men are attacked than women. Nobody knows why.

• More than 90 percent of shark-attack victims survive.

• People who are attacked by sharks are most often bitten on the calf or knee, thighs, or arms. Feet, hands, buttocks, fingers, and toes are the next most common targets of attacks.

Shark Attacks: Those Who Survived and Those Who Didn't

No one who has survived a shark attack ever forgets the terrifying experience. Fortunately, most victims do survive to tell their stories.

RODNEY FOX:
PROTECTING THE JAWS THAT BIT YOU

Australian diver Rodney Fox is one of the most famous shark attack survivors—*and* most famous shark protectors—in the world. Amazingly, it was the attack on him that led to his pioneering campaign to study and protect great white sharks.

It happened December 8, 1963, when Fox, then 22 years old, was competing in the South Australian Spearfishing Championships at Aldinga Bay, Australia. The goal of the competition was to capture the greatest variety of local fishes.

Forty divers had been spearing fish for about four hours, and there was a lot of fish blood in the water. Fox, like the other divers, had a buoy attached by a 30-foot line to his weight belt. The reigning champion, Fox was looking for a dusky morwong, a large, perchlike fish that he thought would help him win the championship again. He was snorkeling in deep water about half a mile offshore when he spied a dusky morwong sleeping in the weeds on the bottom. He aimed his spear gun, but never got to fire the shot. Fox describes what happened:

"I was just about to squeeze the trigger when all of a sudden this huge crash hit me in my left side. I knew it must be a great white shark. It knocked the spear gun out of my hand and the mask off my face, and hurled me through the water at great speed." The animal was now holding Fox in its mouth like a dog holds a bone.

Remembering that the eyes are the shark's most vulnerable part, Fox gouged around the animal's head, trying to stick his fingers in its eyes. At that moment, the shark opened its mouth, letting Fox go.

Fox then got a bear hug around the shark's belly so it couldn't bite him. But now he feared he would drown. "I was running out of air and didn't realize that one of my lungs had been punctured."

Using his foot to push off from the shark, Fox quickly swam to the surface and took two or three big gulps of air. Then he looked down on the terrifying sight he will never forget. The shark was swimming right up toward him, mouth wide open!

Fox kicked at the shark's head as hard as he could, but he barely nicked it. Now right alongside Fox, the shark swallowed the buoy attached to his weight belt. The line had a couple of fish that Fox had already killed hanging on it. The shark began to drag Fox through the water. He frantically tried to free himself from the weight belt, but the buckle had spun around to his back and he couldn't reach it. "I was just about to drown and give up when, all of a sudden, the line snapped."

As the shark swam away, Fox managed to get to the surface and yell, "Shark, shark, shark!"

Two men in a small dinghy were already on their way to see what all the disturbance was about. They rolled Fox into the boat and raced toward shore, where a car took him to the hospital. Within an hour of being attacked, Fox was on the operating table. "It was a miracle that I got there in time for the doctors to save me," he says.

Fox's wounds were severe. His stomach, lungs, and rib cage were exposed. Some of his ribs were crushed, and one lung was punctured. It took four hours of surgery and 462 stitches to close his wounds, yet Fox survived. He credits his recovery to his youth, good health, and will to live. Within three months of the attack, he was diving again. A year later, he was spearfishing. His attitude about sharks, however, was forever changed.

Following his attack, Fox says that some friends—as well as the general public—talked about killing sharks to get revenge on the great white shark that had attacked him. But Fox had no desire to "get back" at anything. He only wanted to learn more about the animals.

Eighteen months after his attack, Fox built the first shark cages ever used to protect those who studied sharks up close. He also organized the first expedition to study great white sharks.

SHARKS OFF NEW JERSEY

One of the most notorious series of shark attacks in U.S. waters occurred during a 12-day period in July 1916 in a place not usually known for shark attacks—New Jersey.

SHARK BYTE!

Experiments show that sharks are attracted to brightly colored objects. Shark researchers use the term "Yum-Yum Yellow" to describe the bright orange, yellow, and orange-yellow colors used internationally for life jackets, rafts, and other sea survival equipment. These colors make the victim of a shipwreck or air crash stand out against the dull background of the sea's surface. But the same colors that make victims visible to rescuers also make them visible to sharks. Colors or materials that reflect a lot of light, such as silver and chrome, also attract the curiosity of sharks.

On July 1, 1916, Charles Vansant, a 25-year-old student, was swimming about 16 yards from shore at Beach Haven, New Jersey, when people on shore spotted a black fin moving toward him.

"Shark! Shark! Get out of the water!" they screamed. If Vansant heard the warning, it was too late. The shark dragged him underwater. A nearby sunbather (who happened to be an Olympic swimmer) raced to help the young man, pulling him to shore. Vansant was taken to the local hospital, but his wounds were so severe that he died the following night.

Five days later, Charles Bruder, a hotel bellboy at Spring Lake, 45 miles north of Beach Haven, was swimming beyond the lifelines—ropes that keep people from swimming out of sight of the lifeguards—when he was attacked. He died on the beach, his legs severed from his body.

Six days later, just twenty miles north of Spring Lake, the nightmare continued. July 12, 1916, was a particularly hot day in Matawan, New Jersey, a small town linked to the Atlantic Ocean by a tidal creek that is only 11 yards across at its widest, but has a channel deep enough for fairly sizable boats to travel through. Trying to keep cool, 12-year-old Lester Stilwell and four of his friends decided to go swimming off an old, dilapidated steamboat pier called Wyckoff Dock on Matawan Creek. They had no idea that less than a thousand yards away, a large black shadow moved quickly upstream in the direction of the swimming hole.

23

Lester, a strong swimmer, floated away from his friends, enjoying the water as he looked up at the sky. Suddenly, Lester's friends saw him disappear underwater, reappear, scream, and disappear again. Lester was known to suffer from seizures, and his friends assumed he was having one. They ran from the water, shouting for help.

A few men came running and dove in the murky water to find Lester. Among them was Stanley Fisher, who stripped to his bathing trunks before diving into the creek. Meanwhile, men in rowboats began plunging oars into the water, feeling for Lester's body.

"I've got him," Fisher shouted as he surfaced. He was holding on to Lester's lifeless body as he swam toward shore. Two men followed in a motorboat. Fisher was standing in waist-deep water when he felt something powerful bump his right leg. Startled, he staggered and yelled. Letting go of Lester's body, Fisher reached for his leg with both hands. But he no longer had a whole right leg. The outside of his thigh, from hip to knee, had been ripped away. Terrified and bleeding heavily, Fisher lost consciousness. The men pulled him into the boat and took him to the pier. He was then carried on a stretcher to the Matawan railroad station. Two hours later, he arrived at a hospital. It was too late. Fisher and Stilwell were now the third and fourth victims of shark attacks in New Jersey waters. In all probability, it was a single shark that killed both Fisher and Stilwell, but whether it was the same shark that had killed Charles Vansant and Charles Bruder earlier that month was never confirmed.

The residents of Matawan were frightened, angry, and determined to kill any shark still swimming in the creek. Within hours, men prepared to set off dynamite charges underwater. But before the first charge was set, a motorboat carrying another victim, 14-year-old Joseph Dunn, pulled up to the pier. Joseph had been on a ladder climbing out of the water several hundred yards downstream from where Lester Stilwell and Stanley Fisher were fatally attacked when a shark grabbed his right leg. While his wounds weren't as severe as the others, most of the flesh below his knee was gone. Joseph was rushed to a local hospital, where doctors saved his leg and his life.

Matawan's shark attacks set off a media frenzy of reporters, photographers, and newsreel cameramen. Suddenly, people reported seeing sharks coming into Matawan Creek with the rising of the ocean's tide, but no shark was ever caught in the creek. Two days after the attacks at Matawan, however, an 8½-foot (2.6-meter) great white shark was caught in Raritan Bay, New Jersey. When the shark was dissected, human flesh and bones were found in its stomach, but no one could determine if they belonged to any of the dead boys. (Today, a DNA analysis could provide conclusive results.)

Experts from the American Museum of Natural History in New York City theorized at the time that the attacks had been made by either a great white or a tiger shark. The only problem was that these sharks rarely swim into fresh water. A more likely culprit was a bull shark, the one species known to frequent both salt water *and* fresh water. Bull sharks have been found in the Mississippi River in the United States, the Mekong River in Vietnam, the Zambezi River in Africa, and Lake Nicaragua in Central America.

AT THE MERCY OF SHARKS

Victims of shipwrecks and air crashes at sea face many perils: drowning, exposure, shock, starvation, and shark attack.

In the mid-1940s, U.S. Navy pilot Lieutenant A. G. Reading and radioman E. H. Almond were flying over the central Pacific Ocean when their small plane developed engine trouble and crashed. Reading was knocked unconscious, but Almond got him out of the sinking plane and inflated Reading's life jacket as well as his own. In the struggle to climb out of the cockpit, Almond's trousers were ripped off. Reading regained consciousness in the water.

Within half an hour, sharks were circling them, but hadn't attacked. An hour went by, and the men heard an airplane. Trying to attract the pilot's attention, Reading and Almond kicked and

DO THEY "BARK" BEFORE THEY BITE?

Some animals use a type of body language called a *threat display* to warn potential predators before they attack. As top predators in the food chain, sharks don't have to threaten. They fear no animal and simply go in for the kill.

Only the gray reef shark is known to threaten before attacking. In this case, the attack is defensive. According to Dr. Don Nelson, this particular shark will make an "exaggerated swimming display" if it is cornered by, say, a diver or one of the small, one-person research submarines that some marine biologists use in their work.

Dr. Nelson, who has been investigating gray reef sharks for about 30 years, has seen the display many times. "The shark swims with [its] back arched, snout raised, and pectoral fins lowered." If divers back off when they see this display, they are not likely to be attacked. If the threat is ignored, says Dr. Nelson, the shark swims in an even more exaggerated way, "fins down, back arched, and with a slow weaving and rolling onto its side, and then streaks in at the intruding object like an arrow being shot out of a bow. Wham, right at you."

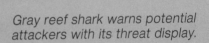

Gray reef shark warns potential attackers with its threat display.

splashed, which only attracted the sharks' attention. Suddenly, Almond felt something grab his right foot. Then he felt pain.

"Get on my back and keep your foot out of the water," Reading told his friend.

As Almond tried to get on Reading's back, the shark struck again and dragged both men underwater. Reading saw five sharks around them and a lot of blood in the water.

He knew they didn't have a chance. Almond's right leg and left thigh were badly bitten. Reading swung his binoculars, which were still hanging around his neck, at passing sharks, but they struck again. Then Reading became separated from Almond. He saw the sharks bite Almond's body. Reading drifted away. Although sharks continued to swim close by, they did not strike him. From time to time, Reading felt a shark brush his foot, but he was not attacked. Many hours later, Reading was rescued by a Navy boat. Almond's body was never found.

Why did the sharks attack Almond but ignore Reading? It is impossible to say for certain, but when Almond lost his trousers, his bare white legs were contrasted against his dark clothing. Sharks are known to be attracted to contrasting colors.

SHARKS IN A FRENZY

What may be one of the worst World War II disasters involving shark attacks occurred on November 28, 1942, when a German submarine torpedoed the British steamship *Nova Scotia* off the coast of South Africa. There were 900 men onboard, including 750 Italian prisoners of war. Some of the men suffered injuries in the explosion and bled into the water. The blood attracted several sharks. One of the survivors described what happened next as a feeding frenzy. In this disaster, the sharks treated the wounded men as prey animals. Many huge sharks joined in the frenzy, biting and ripping flesh from the screaming men.

After 67 hours in the water, 192 survivors were rescued by a Portuguese ship. Sharks were still swimming in the area. The Portuguese sailors fended off the animals with boat hooks as they helped the survivors onboard.

A LOVE-HATE RELATIONSHIP WITH SHARKS

High on the cliffs above Umhlanga (um-LON-guh) Rocks Lighthouse on the Indian Ocean, nine miles north of Durban, the capital of Natal Province, South Africa, sits the headquarters of the Natal Shark Board. Today, the board is a combination scientific laboratory and museum, but its original mission was to protect bathers at Natal's beaches from sharks.

Between December 18, 1957, and January 9, 1958, the South African resort town of Uvongo Beach in Natal was terrorized by five shark attacks. Hysterical tourists fled and a massive anti-shark campaign went into effect. The South African Navy minesweeper *Pretoria* was ordered to kill or frighten off any sharks in the area by dropping explosive depth charges and throwing hand grenades in the waters off the beaches. Uvongo Beach's officials offered rewards to shark hunters to kill sharks. The people of Uvongo Beach meant business.

SHARK ATTACKS BOAT

Sharks are known to attack boats and sometimes bite large chunks out of hulls and oars. The white shark in particular is known to be a boat biter. It especially likes fishing boats, most likely because of the odor of dead fish. Small fishing boats have actually been sunk by sharks.

A basking shark—the second-largest fish in the world, which can grow up to 40 feet long and weigh as much as 16 tons—once attacked a 664-ton steamer carrying 200 passengers. The ship was not damaged, and none of the passengers were wounded, but some became hysterical with fright.

Nobody knows why sharks attack boats. One theory is that the shark's sensitivity to electrical fields may be involved. The boat's electrical fields may resemble those of prey animals.

By April 1958, protective nets had been installed around bathing areas along Natal's coasts, and hotel managers and city councils tried to reassure jittery tourists that it was safe to swim at Natal's beaches.

Fay Bester, a 28-year-old mother of four, was one of many tourists who felt Uvongo Beach was safe again. She was taking her first vacation since her husband had been killed 11 months earlier in a motorcycle accident. On April 5, 1958, Fay and several other hotel guests went for a walk along the beach to see where the protective shark nets were undergoing routine maintenance repairs. At the mouth of a river that fed into the sea, they cooled their feet in the water, going in no deeper than their knees. Suddenly, a six-foot shark swam out of the river channel, rushed Fay, and knocked her into the water. Before anyone could even react, the shark clamped its jaws around Fay's waist and shook her violently. The onlookers screamed and splashed, driving the shark away; but it was too late. Fay was dead, her body bitten almost in half.

The attack triggered mass panic. Cars jammed the roads for miles as tourists fled the area. Within a few months, many hotels in the area went bankrupt. The tourist industry was crippled for almost a year until more effective nets were installed. However, the government felt that more than nets was needed.

In 1964, the Natal Anti-Shark Measures Board (known today as the Natal Shark Board) became the official organization responsible for protecting bathers. Nets put up by the board trap and kill about 1,100 sharks every year. Dolphins, turtles, and seabirds, however, also get caught in the nets and die. As a possible alternative, Natal scientists are trying to develop an electrical shark repellent that will protect as effectively as the nets, with less damage to wildlife.

How *Not* to Photograph a Shark

In 1978, Mike deGruy, a Los Angeles producer of natural history films, traveled to the Marshall Islands in the western Pacific Ocean to work on a film about sharks. On this particular day, he was filming at Eniwetok (en-uh-WEE-tahk), a ring of tiny coral islands in the Marshall chain where the U.S. had tested atomic and hydrogen bombs in the late 1940s and early '50s. Underwater, deGruy was working near a pinnacle reef, a column that came up from the bottom of a 200-foot lagoon. It was a good place to film sharks because a lot of fish came to the reef to feed, and the abundance of fish attracted sharks.

DeGruy and a partner were photographing gray reef sharks about 19 feet away when he noticed one swimming in a weird way with back arched and sideways motions that deGruy recognized as a threat posture, a kind of body language that some animals use to frighten a predator. The men knew that swimming toward a posturing gray reef shark would be dangerous, but didn't think that taking its *picture* would cause any problems. They were wrong.

"Immediately, the shark broke its awkward posture, turned, and began swimming directly toward me at high speed," deGruy said. He didn't have time to reach for his bang stick—an anti-shark club with an explosive attached—so he shoved his camera into the shark's face. The shark knocked the camera aside. "It grabbed the top of my right arm and ripped into it, shaking its body and head. . . . Then it tore a chunk of rubber out of my fin, charged my diving partner, ripped open his hand, and swam away. We were left with the long ordeal of getting back to the boat."

Both divers were taken to the U.S. Navy Hospital in Guam, and later transferred to Honolulu for surgery, where both fully recovered. DeGruy continues making films about sharks, animals that he still respects and admires, but he no longer sets off flashes close to posturing gray reef sharks. Dr. Don Nelson, professor of marine biology at California State, believes that gray reef sharks launch such attacks to scare off what the sharks think is an enemy.

THE ATTACK THAT SHOULD HAVE HAPPENED

Sharks are normally cautious. Some are even shy, but they will come after anything that sounds or smells like fish. While using a dead fish to bait sharks during a film assignment, marine biologist and shark expert Rocky Strong and his cameramen came close to becoming bait themselves.

It happened in a shallow lagoon in French Frigate Shoals, Hawaii, in 1989. To attract a shark within camera range, Strong put an ultrasonic transmitter inside half a fish and dropped it into the water on a piece of string attached to a floating hand reel. The idea was to get a shark to swallow the fish containing the transmitter so its movements could be followed by the researchers.

Strong, cameraman Mike deGruy (featured in previous story), and assistant cameraman Chip Matheson stationed themselves underwater to wait and see what would happen. They were not in shark cages and, for some reason, were not wearing protective stainless steel shark suits, which lay in their boat 30 feet away.

A gray reef shark snatched the fish half and swam away before deGruy could take a picture. DeGruy spotted a group of 18 pregnant female gray reef sharks milling peacefully some distance away. He suggested trying to attract one of them to photograph instead.

Strong took the other fish half, which also contained a transmitter and was connected to a line attached to another fishing reel. DeGruy turned on the camera. They were within 30 feet of the pregnant females when Strong saw one animal flinch. Immediately, he knew that the current must be carrying the fish odor toward the sharks. He told deGruy they needed to hurry because the sharks were catching the fish's scent. Suddenly, two or three sharks made turning motions. Within seconds, all the sharks turned at once. "They launched at us like rockets," Strong says. He knew a feeding frenzy was forming around them.

At that moment, holding the half fish was as dangerous as holding a live hand grenade, and Strong tried his best to get rid of it. Standing with his head above the surface, he threw the fish as hard as he could. The line snagged, and the fish fell right in front of the three men. The water was so shallow at this point that Strong, deGruy, and Matheson were standing with their heads above the surface, looking down on a terrifying sight. Sharks were zooming all around them. "It was like being in a school of huge piranhas," Strong said. "We stepped in close and huddled together with our backs against each other." One shark leapt out of the water and landed right between Strong's and deGruy's shoulders. Then Strong saw the hand reel that was attached to the line holding the fish move quickly across the surface of the water. A shark had grabbed the fish and swum away. All at once, the other sharks followed.

"What amazes me to this day is why one of us didn't get bitten," Strong says. He admits that being in the water with a dead fish was not a good idea.

SHARK BYTE!

At times, some sharks depart from their normal diets and devour a variety of land animals, including dogs, cats, and cattle. In Australia, sharks have even attacked racehorses being exercised in the surf.

The most unusual shark attack recorded was made in 1959 on an elephant. The creature, believed to be suffering from extreme thirst, charged into the ocean off Kenya, Africa, apparently in search of fresh water on a nearby island. The elephant, however, never reached the island. Sharks attacked and ate it as horrified onlookers watched from shore.

SCOOTING TO DANGER

The Pacific Ocean off northern California is a known hangout for great white sharks. Every diver knows this and hopes never to run into one. But sometimes it happens. On June 30, 1995, it happened to 31-year-old Marco Flagg.

Flagg and several others were scuba-diving in 90 feet of calm water about 200 yards off Blue Fish Cove, a popular dive site in the waters off Point Lobos State Reserve, just south of Carmel, California. Flagg was riding a small underwater electric scooter and was about 50 feet down when he saw a huge white shark about 20 feet away.

As calmly as he could, he turned the scooter and headed back toward the boat, moving at a steady rate and a shallow ascent angle. As a trained diver, he knew he couldn't just pop up to the surface. Nitrogen gas that builds up in body tissues during a dive can cause life-threatening problems—called the bends—if a diver returns to the surface too quickly.

About 20 seconds later, Flagg saw the shark again. This time, its massive, wide-open mouth was coming right at him. A second later, he felt a dull pressure on his body and knew the shark was biting him.

But as quickly as it had attacked, the shark let go. Flagg felt for his legs to make sure he still had them, then zoomed to the boat as fast as the scooter would go. He was taken to a hospital, where he needed 15 stitches for wounds to his thigh, torso, and shoulder. The unmistakable tooth marks of a great white were left on his air tank.

In this case, marine biologists believe the shark was attracted to the electrical field of the scooter rather than to the diver himself.

Anti-Shark Devices

For more than 50 years, scientists all over the world have tried to develop an effective shark repellent. Various chemical repellents and anti-shark devices have been tried. Most have failed. A few, however, have worked with varying degrees of success.

SHARK CHASER

In 1943, the Navy developed a water-soluble cake known as "Shark Chaser." The cake consisted of a mixture of 80 percent nigrosine dye and 20 percent copper acetate, and was included in a survival packet issued to all Navy and Air Force personnel. Preliminary tests showed that the dye blocked sight and the copper acetate inhibited feeding responses in captive smooth dogfish sharks. But, says George Burgess, director of the International Shark Attack File, in real-life situations, the mixture didn't work once the dye floated away. "Shark Chaser" is no longer in use.

Dilution by the ocean is the major problem in finding an effective chemical shark repellent. "You would need to have barge-loads of chemicals being shoveled into the water to keep sharks away from humans," George Burgess says.

JOHNSON SHARK SCREEN

Devised especially for ocean disaster survivors, this large, foldable plastic bag is named for its inventor, Dr. C. Scott Johnson. It can be carried in a shirt pocket. The survivor of an air or sea disaster simply unfolds the bag, lets it fill with water, and then enters the bag, keeping his or her head above the water's surface. When unfolded, the bag is five feet deep and two to three feet in diameter. Three built-in inflatable flotation rings, colored international orange, are fitted with mouthpieces to enable the survivor to fill them with air. The flotation rings suspend the bag from the surface of the water. The bag protects the survivor by masking shapes, sounds, odors, and electrical fields that might attract sharks. Tests showed that the Johnson Shark Screen effectively protected victims of air or sea disasters awaiting rescue on the surface. It cannot be used to protect a moving swimmer or diver, however.

STAINLESS STEEL CHAIN MAIL SUIT

This garment was developed and tested by pioneering underwater filmmakers Valerie and Ron Taylor. Ron got the idea for the chain mail suit in 1967 while working on a scientific expedition

HOW *NOT* TO ATTRACT A SHARK

The following guidelines were developed by the U.S. Navy and scientists working with the International Shark Attack File. They should be followed when going into any body of water where sharks are found.

• Do not swim or dive alone, and do not isolate yourself from other people in the water. Most attacks are on lone swimmers or surfers.

• Do not swim in waters that are known to be frequented by dangerous sharks.

• Leave the water immediately if a shark is sighted.

• Do not go into the water if you are bleeding from an open wound or menstruating. A shark's sense of smell is extremely keen.

• Do not swim far from shore, where encountering a shark is more probable.

• Be cautious when swimming in areas between sandbars or near channels or steep drop-offs. These are favorite hangouts for sharks.

• Leave the water immediately if you see fish acting strangely.

• Don't swim with an animal, such as a dog or a horse.

• Look carefully for shadows before jumping or diving into the water.

• Use extra caution in murky water, and avoid uneven body tanning that leaves strap or sleeve marks. Sharks see contrast particularly well.

• Avoid wearing bright-colored clothing in the water.

• Do not swim at dusk or at night, when many species of fish, including sharks, hunt for food.

• Avoid waters where garbage or sewage is dumped. Sharks are attracted to these areas to feed.

• Never wear watches or shiny jewelry, buttons, or buckles in the water. They reflect light and resemble the sheen of fish scales, which attracts sharks.

• Never poke or bother a shark, no matter how small.

on Australia's Great Barrier Reef. One member of the expedition team happened to have a pair of steel chain mail, or fine flexible metal mesh, gloves, which were originally designed to keep butchers from cutting their hands with sharp knives. He wore the gloves to clean fish. If a glove could protect hands from knife cuts, thought Ron, why not make a suit to protect divers from sharks?

Working with marine biologist Jeremiah Sullivan, Ron Taylor designed the first steel mesh suit. It weighed 13 pounds, about the same as a diver's weight belt. Valerie Taylor was the first to try the new suit in 1978, during a trip to the Coral Sea. The Taylors put fish in the water to attract the area's gray reef sharks. Both Valerie and Ron waited underwater to see what would happen. The sharks ate the bait and circled Valerie, but they didn't attack her.

In 1980, the Taylors tested the suit with blue sharks off the California coast. Blue sharks are known to have no fear of divers. While Ron filmed, Valerie held a bleeding fish to bait sharks into biting her arm. She described what happened: "A big blue shark caught me unawares and latched on to my arm with a sudden thump. I was, to say the least, startled. . . . As the shock wore off, I realized that there was no blood and that it wasn't really hurting. There was just the initial thump and a squeezed feeling."

Although chain mail suits are available commercially and provide good protection for divers who want to film or study sharks without being confined in a shark cage, the suits are too heavy to be worn by surfers.

SHARK BILLY

A short wooden or plastic pole, about four feet long, carried by most divers. The billy is used not to hit sharks but to push them away. "When a shark approaches or circles in too close to investigate, you

just push it away," says Dr. Don Nelson. He has
given many a shark a nudge during his years of
underwater research. What part of the
shark's body do you push? "It's best at
the snout if the shark is approaching
you head on, or mid-body if it's circling," he says. "What
you're trying to do is discourage them so they'll eventually leave."

POWERHEAD

This device, also called a bang stick or smokey, is armed with an
explosive and is actually a dangerous weapon. On contact with the
shark's body, the powerhead detonates, immobilizing or killing the
shark. This device is extremely sensitive, and several divers have
gotten their hands blown off trying to use it. In some parts of the
world, use of a powerhead is prohibited by law.

CHEMICAL SQUIRT GUN

For divers, one way to avoid the dilution problem is to squirt chemical repellent directly into a shark's mouth (not an impossible feat
when the open mouth of an attacking shark is only a few feet away).
Dr. Don Nelson and his colleagues have been testing a detergent-like
chemical called sodium lauryl sulfate, which acts like a kind of underwater Mace or pepper spray on various species of sharks. "You have to
get at least some of the chemical in the shark's mouth because that
appears to be the sensitive area. They will shake their heads, spit it
out, and dash away with their mouths wide open," he says.

Dr. Nelson has also been involved in developing chemical repellent cartridges that divers could carry on their belts. One cartridge
can be screwed onto the head of a shark billy. The billy, along with
a backup cartridge, can be carried on the diver's belt. A marketable
version of a chemical repellent gun is still in the development phase.

Netting

Since 1937, nylon fishing nets have been strung off resort beaches in Australia, and since 1952 in South Africa, to protect swimmers from sharks. The nets are very effective. Every year, though, thousands of sharks, dolphins, turtles, and seabirds get tangled in the nets and drown. Scientists and conservationists are currently looking for other ways to protect beaches from sharks, such as gaining greater knowledge of shark behavior and use of electrical devices.

Protective Ocean Device (POD)

This newest shark repellent was developed by scientists at the Natal Shark Board. It surrounds the wearer with a 120-volt electrical field, strong enough to repel large dangerous sharks, such as the great white and bull shark, without hurting the diver. POD operates on batteries and is about the size of a thermos bottle. The POD model that is currently available straps onto the diver's air tank and has a foot probe that is attached to one of the diver's fins. The switch, which is connected to the POD on the diver's back and brought over his or her shoulder, remains on throughout the dive because most victims don't see the shark until it strikes. In the future, POD may be built into surfboards, sailboards, bodyboards, life jackets, and perhaps can be designed to protect entire bathing areas at beaches.

POD is available to divers through the Natal Shark Board.

Anti-Shark Cage

Suspended from a ship, the heavy metal shark cage hangs underwater, where it is used by scientists and film crews working in shark-infested waters. The cage has open bars that are too strong for a shark to break and too close together for a shark to swim through. Shark cages vary in size from a two-person cage to one that holds six or more people.

SPECIES

"There are many different species of sharks, and the majority of them are scavengers. Their job is to pick up garbage—the leftovers and the dead and wounded. Sharks keep the ocean clean, just as garbage collectors keep the cities clean."

Jean-Michel Cousteau, ocean explorer

OF THE 350-PLUS SPECIES OF SHARKS, only about 30 are considered dangerous to humans. Of these 30, three species—the great white shark, the tiger shark, and the bull shark—account for the most fatalities.

The Three Most Wanted

WHITE SHARK

Commonly known as the great white shark, this animal is the largest and most feared of the flesh-eating sharks. Great whites normally range from 16 to 21 feet in length and weigh between 1 and 3 tons. But larger ones have been caught. The largest great white actually measured was 29.5 feet long and weighed an estimated 10,000 pounds (5 tons)! Australians call the great white "white pointer" or "white death." Its name comes from its white belly; its back is black. Found in every ocean on earth, the great white favors cool, temperate waters, such as the Pacific Coast off northern California, the offshore waters of southern Africa, and southern and western Australia. It is rare in tropical waters.

Many marine biologists consider the white shark the most dangerous fish in the ocean, and more attacks on humans have been attributed to it than to any other species. The white shark accounts for the great majority, if not all, of the attacks on humans in waters off the coasts of central and north-ern California and southern Australia.

White sharks normally feed on a variety of bony fishes such as tuna, other sharks, dolphins, har-bor seals, sea lions, and elephant seals. White sharks also feed on garbage and dead animals. According to Dr. Peter Klimley of Bodega Marine Laboratory in Bodega Bay, California, the white shark "may find human prey unpalatable." The white shark's pre-ferred foods—seals and whales—are made mostly of fat, but birds, sea otters, and people are mainly muscle. This might be why white sharks often bite a human once, then let go and swim away.

Dr. John McCosker of the Steinhart Aquarium in San Francisco, California, conducted experiments to test the white shark's response to dummies dressed like divers in wet suits. He placed some of the dummies in an upright position on the ocean floor. Others were attached to surfboards with their legs and arms hanging off the sides. The sharks were not interested in the upright dummies on the bot-tom unless bait was attached to them. The dummies on surfboards were immediately attacked, suggesting that a person lying on a surf-board may resemble a seal, which white sharks normally eat.

The white shark usually attacks its prey by surprise from behind and below. Swimming at 10 to 15 miles per hour, the shark may suddenly rush prey. High-speed photography taken near Dangerous Reef, Australia, reveals the steps in capturing the prey below.

1. normal jaw position

2. shark raises snout and lowers jaw

3. upper jaw protrudes, lower jaw moves upward, grasping prey

4. protruded jaw slides back into normal position

The white shark is the only shark that lifts its head clear out of the water to look at objects on the surface. But when a great white bites, it can't see its prey because its eyes roll backward in their sockets. Scientists think this adaptation evolved as a way of avoiding injury from the teeth and claws of struggling seals and sea lions.

BULL SHARK

The bull shark is one of the most dangerous sharks to humans in tropical and subtropical waters. It grows up to 11 feet in length and has huge jaws and large, sharp teeth. Its back is gray and its underbelly off-white. Large prey, including other sharks, dolphins, and sea turtles, are its main food, but the bull shark will eat almost anything. It has even been known to kill hippopotamuses in African rivers. Bull sharks are responsible for most attacks on bathers at South African beaches.

The bull shark is the only shark species that can live in both fresh and salt water. In August 1985, a bull shark was caught in Chesapeake Bay. A bull shark may have been responsible for the famous attacks that occurred in 1916 off the New Jersey coast and in Matawan Creek. (See story on page 23.)

TIGER SHARK

The tiger shark is the third shark considered dangerous to humans. Grayish black with tigerlike stripes across its back that fade in adulthood, the tiger shark is a large, powerful, fierce predator. Adults can grow up to 19 feet long. Especially abundant in the Caribbean Sea and in the Pacific Ocean near Hawaii, the tiger swims close to shore, sometimes venturing into bays or near wharves. It will attack anything that floats and is the junk food eater of the shark kingdom. Everything, from seals and dolphins to cans of paint, has been found in tiger sharks' stomachs.

Every summer, however, some tiger sharks depart from their usual diet of lobsters, turtles, and seals. They arrive at the northwestern Hawaiian Islands just at the time albatross chicks are beginning to fly. During a two-week period, these sharks ignore the seals and turtles that are swimming all around them and feast only on the little birds that fall into the ocean.

Other Dangerous Sharks

While not as large as the three supersharks, the following sharks are known to be ferocious predators, and have occasionally been known to attack humans.

SHARK HITCHHIKERS

Who'd want to hitch a ride on a shark? A remora, that's who. These small fish attach themselves to sharks via a suction disk on the top of their heads. Both the shark and the remora benefit from this relationship: the shark because the remora cleans parasites from its body and inside its mouth; the remora because it feasts on parasites and leftovers in the shark's teeth and gets a free ride wherever the shark may roam. This is called mutualism, a relationship in which two different organisms both benefit.

BLACKTIP REEF SHARK

The blacktip reef shark is gray with black tips on its fins. It grows to about seven feet long and is found in tropical and subtropical waters throughout the Pacific and Indian oceans, the Red Sea, and the eastern Mediterranean. It frequents shallow waters, sometimes only a few *inches* deep, where people are wading and swimming. It has also been known to attack people in areas where speared fish are hanging on lines or where people are cleaning fish.

GRAY REEF SHARK

The gray reef shark, which grows to an average length of five to six feet, is common throughout the rings of tiny coral islands, such as the Marshall Islands, the Caroline Islands, and the Gilbert Islands, in the tropical Pacific. It is the only shark known to have a recognizable threat posture. If divers don't back off when the gray reef shark displays this posture, they can be attacked and seriously injured, even killed.

Shortfin Mako

The shortfin mako, with its metallic blue back and white under-belly, is prized by game fishermen. When hooked, it can leap 20 feet into the air, and has been known to jump into the very fishing boat that is pursuing it.

The shortfin mako is found worldwide but is most abundant in the Atlantic Ocean. It may be the fastest of all sharks. It holds the speed record for long-distance travel: 1,322.7 miles in 37 days, or an average of about 36 miles per day.

The shortfin mako's favorite food is bluefish, but it will eat other sea animals. People who like to eat shark consider shortfin mako the most delicious shark meat.

This shark usually keeps to offshore waters, far beyond the range of most swimmers and divers.

Blue Shark

The blue shark gets its name from the brilliant blue color of its sides and back; its belly is white. It is the most common shark of the open ocean off the east and west coasts of the United States. It is also the most widely traveled species. Scientists have tagged some blue sharks with identification numbers and kept records on them. When a tagged individual is recovered, sometimes years later, scientists check their data to learn how far the shark traveled. The record distance is held by a blue shark that swam 3,740 miles from New York to Brazil, providing the first evidence that blue sharks from the western Atlantic cross the equator.

The blue shark usually feeds on squid and small bony fishes such as mackerel and bluefish. They have been known to attack humans and boats. Feeding frenzies of blue sharks are often seen around whale carcasses.

Shark Lovers ♥ RON AND VALERIE TAYLOR

The Australian diving couple Ron and Valerie Taylor have spent more time in the water with sharks than probably any other people in the world. In 1965, Ron Taylor became the first person to film a great white shark underwater. While hanging unprotected from a platform at the back of a tuna boat, he shot the footage. Today, more than 30 years later, the Taylors are still filming great whites and other sharks.

Filmmaking has often provided the Taylors with an opportunity to learn something new about sharks and their intelligence. Once they were filming a tiger shark for a New Zealand film called The Silent One. The tiger shark had been caught by a local diver and brought to a lagoon separated from the open ocean by a steel mesh fence. Valerie Taylor stationed herself in the ocean outside the fence and took photographs of the shark as it circled inside the lagoon. It swam around and around, circling. Valerie knew the shark was looking for a way out of the lagoon. While observing the shark, she saw a large fish called a sole trying to get out at the base of the fence. When Valerie scooped away enough sand to free the sole, the tiger shark immediately took notice. After the sole swam free, the tiger shark swam down to the little excavation and tried to fit its snout into the gap and under the fence. Valerie was very impressed by this shark's intelligence.

"Sharks, even the so-called dangerous ones, are far more intelligent than is generally believed. If handled in the right way, they will perform in a manner that shows that they have at least as much ability to comprehend a situation as many land animals do," she says in the book Sharks: Silent Hunters of the Deep, published in Australia.

Strange and Unusual Sharks

HAMMERHEAD SHARK

Hammerhead sharks have the most unusual heads of any animal in the sea. Their head looks like a hammer or a double-bladed ax. The shark's eyes are more than a foot apart, one on each tip of its hammerhead! The nostrils, too, are widely spaced. The widest head in proportion to body size belongs to the species commonly called the wingspread shark. The width of its head is half the length of its five-foot body.

There are eight species of hammerhead sharks. The largest is the great hammerhead, which can grow up to 20 feet long. The smallest, the bonnethead, reaches about five feet and is harmless to humans.

Hammerheads are found around the world in shallow ocean waters close to coastlines. The three largest species are the smooth hammerhead, the scalloped hammerhead, and the great hammerhead, which is found in warm waters along the coasts of Central and South America, Australia, and Africa.

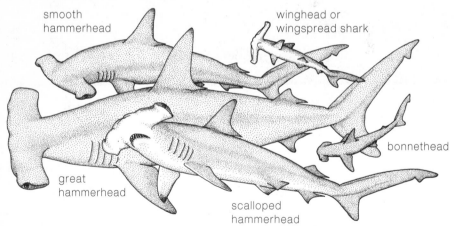

smooth hammerhead

winghead or wingspread shark

bonnethead

great hammerhead

scalloped hammerhead

WHALE SHARK

The whale shark is the world's largest fish—and possibly the most gentle member of the shark family. Its name refers to its size, which

47

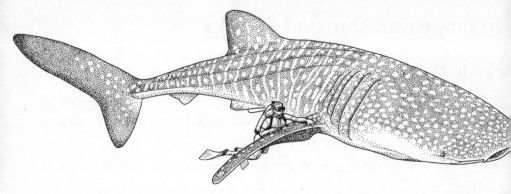

is about the same as sperm and humpback whales. It may reach up to 59 feet in length (more than half the length of a basketball court) and weigh more than 21 tons. Although whale sharks are monstrous in size, they feed on the tiniest creatures in the ocean—microscopic drifting organisms called plankton. When feeding, whale sharks swim with their mouth open and filter plankton from the water.

Whale sharks are not dangerous to humans, but their large size means that divers must be careful to keep a distance from their powerful fins and tail. Whale sharks are so gentle that many divers have hitched rides on them.

Megamouth

Just as marine biologists were beginning to think all living shark species had been identified, a new one was found. It wasn't a small one, either. In 1976, a huge, unidentifiable shark was caught by accident in a Hawaiian fisherman's net. Almost 15 feet long, with dusky brown to black skin, the creature represented a new family and species of shark. Scientists rushed to examine the animal, then spent seven years studying the specimen before officially naming it in 1983, when the first description of it was published. As you might guess, the megamouth is named for its big mouth, which is lined with silvery tissue. Its scientific name, *Megachasma* (meg-uh-KAZ-muh), comes from a Greek word meaning large, open mouth. During the day, megamouths stay in the deep ocean and feed on krill, tiny shrimplike animals. At night, they follow the krill as they migrate upward to 40 feet below the surface. There, the megamouths feed again.

The only megamouth specimen in the world on display is at the Los Angeles County Museum of Natural History in Los Angeles, California. It was caught in 1984 off Santa Catalina Island, California. Fewer than a dozen specimens of this shark have been caught worldwide. It is unknown how many are alive today.

DOGFISH SHARK

The smallest sharks are found in the dogfish family. They are called "dogfish" because they gather in large "packs," sometimes consisting of thousands of fish.

SHARK BYTE!

Unlike humans, sharks continue to grow in size throughout their lives. For the spiny dogfish, this may be 70 to 100 years! Whale sharks may live 60 years.

Working as a pack, they attack schools of prey species, including larger fish such as cod and halibut. Spiny dogfish also feed on small bony fish, worms, squid, and other invertebrates—animals without backbones.

The deep-water dwarf dog shark, found in the Caribbean Sea off Colombia, South America, reaches only about seven inches in length. The cigar shark (named for its shape) grows to about nine inches in length. It—like the dwarf dog shark—stays in deep water during the day, but migrates closer to the surface at night to feed on tiny squid and lanternfishes. These tiny dogfish sharks are harmless to humans.

SPINY DOGFISH

This small, slate gray shark is the most well-studied of all sharks. Spiny dogfish are easy to catch and are commonly dissected in college biology courses to teach students fish anatomy. They are also used in biomedical research to study the sharks' immune system and, in particular, to learn why they don't get cancer. At maturity, female spiny dogfish reach 27 to 48 inches long; males are smaller, 23 to 39 inches. Spiny dogfish are the most numerous and commercially important sharks in the world.

Spiny dogfish are processed into fish meal, which is used to feed livestock and to make the oil found in cat and dog food.

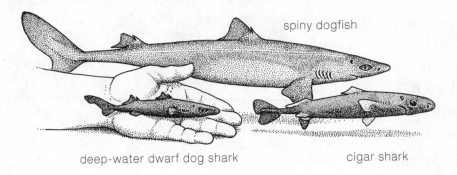

spiny dogfish

deep-water dwarf dog shark   cigar shark

CULTURE SHARK

"When I first began diving, 30 years ago, fear of shark attack was my constant companion. The media, with its lurid and often inaccurate accounts of shark attacks, had conditioned me—along with everyone else—into believing that sharks were monstrous killers. . . . My attitude toward the sea and its inhabitants has now changed completely, particularly where sharks are concerned. What I once feared, I now respect."

Valerie Taylor, professional diver/photographer

THROUGHOUT HISTORY, people have used sharks as they have many other animals—for food, experimentation, even medicinal purposes. With tens of thousands of sharks being fished annually throughout the world and thousands more accidentally trapped in nets, there is certainly cause for concern. Many marine biologists, divers, and environmentalists are worried that shark populations are being seriously depleted worldwide. Scientists believe that without sharks, the oceans could become overpopulated, particularly with weaker and sick fish, creating an unhealthy environment.

Sharks for Food

Worldwide, the major use of sharks today is for human consumption. Commercial shark fishing developed in the 1970s. Although shark meat has never been a popular food in the United States, it is widely eaten in other parts of the world, especially China, Japan, and the South Sea Islands. The demand for shark meat will probably increase as people turn more to the sea to feed the growing human population.

The best-known edible part of the shark is its fins. Shark-fin soup, or *yerchee*, is a classic Chinese dish. Fins from the school shark are so prized for soup that this species is often called the "soupfin shark."

The finning business is worth more than $500 million per year. Fishermen can get up to $200 per pound for shark fins. In Asia, a single bowl of shark-fin soup can cost as much as $50.

Fishermen usually cut off the shark's fins, then throw the shark back into the sea, where it bleeds to death.

To prepare fins for market, fishermen remove the skin and muscular tissue, keeping only the cartilaginous rods that support the fin. The

CALLING ALL SHARKS

Today, in some western Pacific island villages, such as those on Kiribati, Tonga, and the Trobriand Islands, young men must prove their masculinity by calling a shark to swim close to their boat and catching the animal with a rope. This custom is called shark calling and is an ancient technique.

The shark caller's equipment consists of a wooden float attached to a long rope and a cane hoop some three feet in diameter. Threaded onto the hoop are about 20 disks cut from coconut shells. To call a shark, the hoop is held partially underwater and shaken vigorously.

If a shark comes over to investigate the noise, the hunter ties a slipknot on the rope attached to the float, creating a noose. Dipping a fish on a stick into the water, the hunter then tries to lure the shark into putting its head through the noose. If the shark takes the bait, the hunter pulls the rope tight over its gills, which makes it impossible for the shark to breathe. Then he patiently waits until the shark stops struggling. Carefully he paddles his canoe to the float, pulls the shark's head out of the water, and kills it with the sharp blows of a club.

rods are then pressed into disks about nine inches in diameter and a half inch thick. It is these disks that are used to make shark-fin soup.

In Japan, mako steak and shark teriyaki are popular. The dish known as *kamaboko*, which is famous in Japan, is made from crushed shark flesh, cornstarch, and other ingredients, which are shaped into a kind of pancake and steamed or roasted. One can find mako steak on the menus of some restaurants in the United States.

Sharks for Medicine

During the 1940s, there was a kind of gold rush on sharks' livers. At the height of the boom, sharks' livers brought $14.25 per pound and supplied three-fourths of the vitamin A produced in the United States. The military was particularly interested in vitamin A for its ability to prevent night blindness, a condition that makes it difficult to see in dim light. Night blindness is particularly dangerous for soldiers, as many military maneuvers are carried out under the cover of darkness.

Shark-liver oil was also used in the 1940s for tanning leather, soap-making, and tempering high-grade steel. When scientists learned to create vitamin A in the laboratory in the 1950s, the shark oil industry nearly collapsed. Today, shark-liver oil can be found in cosmetics, special lubricants for machine parts, and listed as an ingredient in popular over-the-counter hemorrhoid ointments.

MODERN REMEDIES

Sharks do not get cancer. People want to learn why. Medical researchers suspect a substance naturally found in shark cartilage may hold the key to the mystery.

- Scientists are testing an extract from shark cartilage in hopes that it can be used to treat or prevent cancers and various other diseases in people, including arthritis, psoriasis, and eczema.

- Chondroitin (kon-DRO-uh-tin), a substance from shark cartilage, is being tested for making artificial skin for burn patients.

- A substance found in the liver of the dogfish shark may slow the growth of brain tumors. Scientists at Johns Hopkins Medical Institutions found that the substance, squalene (SKWAH-leen), nearly stops the growth of new blood vessels that feed solid brain tumors in laboratory animals. No tests on whether the substance can help people with brain tumors have been performed yet.

- Shark corneas have been used as replacements for human corneas.

Sharks and Hollywood

Peter Benchley's 1974 novel *Jaws*, and the movie of the same name that followed, set off a tidal wave of shark hysteria unlike anything since the public outcry following the 1916 shark attacks in New Jersey. *Jaws* is the story of a shark that terrorizes the beaches of the fictional East Coast resort town Amity. The movie had theater audiences screaming in horror, and people were suddenly afraid to go into the water. Books, magazine articles, and news reports on sharks appeared everywhere. Like the wolf in "Little Red Riding Hood," the big, bad shark became a symbol, representing people's ancient fear of the monsters they imagined swam in the dark, alien world of the sea. Suddenly, every shark attack made front-page headlines, usually with a picture of a wide-open, toothy mouth sticking out of the water. Little attempt was made to report how rarely attacks took place. The media, essentially, was in a feeding frenzy.

Jaws was directed by then 26-year-old Steven Spielberg. He sent a crew to Australia to film real white sharks for some scenes in the movie, but the film's "star" was not a real shark. It was a mechanical model (or actually, *three* 24-foot, one-and-a-half-ton polyurethane

54

PROTECTING
THE GREAT WHITE

In 1991, South Africa made history by declaring the white shark an endangered species —the first country in the world to do so. In 1994, California prohibited both sport and commercial fishing of the white in its waters. There are also limits on the number of blue, leopard, thresher, and shortfin mako sharks that can be caught in California waters. Since 1992, it has been illegal to catch basking, saw, and whale sharks in Florida's waters. In 1996, the U.S. National Marine Fisheries Service (NMFS) proposed a ban on fishing for white, whale, and basking sharks in the Atlantic Ocean and the Gulf of Mexico.

The Australian government has given official protection to Dangerous Reef, a tiny island off the southern coast of Australia that is known for the great white sharks that live in its waters. Shark scientists hope that other countries with white sharks will follow these examples.

sharks, all nicknamed Bruce, costing $150,000 each). The first Bruce sank to the bottom of Nantucket Sound during production of the movie. The second exploded. The surviving Bruce couldn't close its jaws properly, but it was the one seen in the movie.

Operating Bruce was quite a chore. First, a 12-ton steel platform had to be sunk to the ocean floor to provide a space for Bruce's underwater handlers to work. Then the mechanical shark was attached to the platform by a 100-foot cable. Each time a scene with Bruce was shot, it took 13 scuba-diving technicians to operate the controls on the underwater platform.

Bruce also needed makeup. A special makeup man in scuba gear dove into the ocean from time to time to apply fake blood to Bruce's teeth and gums.

Although Bruce was just a big piece of plastic, he succeeded in scaring the bejeebers out of otherwise rational people all over the world. He also drew crowds. The movie *Jaws* has made $458 million worldwide and ranks among the highest-grossing films of all time. It was followed by three sequels: *Jaws 2*, *Jaws 3-D*, and *Jaws the Revenge*.

TAKE A RIDE ON *JAWS*

Want to feel as if you're being attacked by a shark . . . without the wear and tear on your bod? Universal Studios in Orlando, Florida, has created a *Jaws* ride, open to the public. A five-million-gallon, seven-acre lagoon was constructed to look just like the bay in the original *Jaws* movie. Visitors ride in a boat that is repeatedly attacked by a 32-foot shark made of steel and fiberglass with realistic latex skin and urethane teeth. With underwater technology never used before in any other attraction in the world, the shark moves at 20 feet per second (about the same speed as a car traveling at 15 miles per hour), thrusting with power equal to the jet engine of a Boeing 727 airplane!

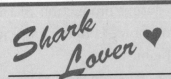 **EUGENIE CLARK**

Dr. Eugenie Clark has ridden on the back of a whale shark, dived into underwater caves and discovered "sleeping" sharks, and swum unprotected, side by side with dangerous sharks, numerous times. She is not afraid. She loves sharks.

Dr. Clark became fascinated with sharks at the age of nine when she visited the New York Aquarium. She told people then that one day she would swim with sharks. Years later, she went to college and became an ichthyologist—a scientist who studies fishes. She also became a diver and has been diving for more than 45 years. Now in her sixties, she is a professor in the department of zoology at the University of Maryland.

In the late 1950s, as director and founder of the Cape Haze Marine Laboratory (now called the Mote Marine Lab) in Sarasota, Florida, Dr. Clark conducted experiments proving that sharks are smarter than people had originally thought. In laboratory experiments conducted by Dr. Clark, lemon sharks learned to perform certain tasks such as ringing a bell to get food. Other sharks in her experiments learned to tell the difference between square and diamond shapes, and between vertical and horizontal stripes.

In the late 1980s, Dr. Clark became interested in studying deep-sea sharks, a variety of species living well below the ocean surface. To observe these animals close-up, she descended into the ocean in a submersible—a small vehicle that carries one or two divers to depths too deep to reach in only scuba gear. Her submersible was once surrounded by 21 sharks. The sharks were swimming with their mouths open in response to the scientist's bait, and one female shark inadvertently swam into a male's mouth. Just as quickly, she swam out unharmed, but bearing toothmarks on her head where the male had instinctively clamped down. Both sharks were about 12 feet long. "It was a very dramatic sight," said Dr. Clark.

One of Dr. Clark's most well-known discoveries is the shark-repelling secretion of a little flatfish from the Red Sea known as the Moses sole. Dr. Clark found that the Moses sole secretes a milky white liquid that contains the toxin pardaxin. This chemical, which is similar to detergents used in the home, affects the gills of sharks. Although the fish uses its secretion to keep sharks away, when the substance is collected from the Moses sole and freeze-dried, it loses its strength quickly and is diluted in the open sea.

SHARKING CAREERS

"We try to get the message across that we have to protect the sharks and all of nature's animals, for the sake of our earth. If we don't, it'll all disappear."

Rodney Fox, shark attack survivor and shark advocate

DO YOU FIND FISH FASCINATING? Would you like to work in the ocean, aboard research ships or on underwater dives? If so, a career as a marine biologist might be for you. Marine biologists do a variety of jobs. Some work as curators in natural history museums. Some do research for pharmaceutical companies looking for new medicines from the sea. Some work for oil companies trying to locate underwater oil supplies. Many teach in universities. What can you do *now* to prepare for a career in marine biology?

• Take all the high school biology and math courses you can, and two foreign language courses.

• Become computer literate.

• Take courses in English composition and learn to express your ideas in writing. Scientists are expected to write and publish research papers about their work.

• Try to get some firsthand experience by volunteering as a summer research assistant or intern at a local natural history museum, aquarium, or marine science institute.

• Apply to a college with a strong biology department, preferably one with a lot of courses in marine biology. Ichthyology, the study of fishes, is the branch of biology that deals with sharks. You will need *three* university degrees if you want to be a research scientist—an undergraduate (bachelor's) degree, or B.S., in biology; an M.S. (a master's degree), and a Ph.D. Research scientists work at universities or medical institutions, or in the field. They try to discover new information about sharks, such as how they mate, what distances they travel, and why they don't get cancer.

• Curiosity and good observational skills are essential for science. There is still much we don't know about sharks, particularly the larger species, such as the bull, tiger, and great white. For more information, request the brochure "Careers in Ichthyology" from:

American Society of Ichthyologists and Herpetologists
Texas Natural History Collection
University of Texas/R4000, Austin, Texas 78712-1100
Phone: (512) 471-0998 FAX: (512) 471-9775
e-mail: asih@mail.utexas.edu
ASIH WWW: http://www.utexas.edu/depts/asih

Sources on Sharks

VIDEOS

To observe attacking sharks from the safety of your living room, check out these high-quality videos. They're available at video stores with good selections of nature documentaries, and they can be ordered from any large bookstore.

The Great White Shark: Lonely Lord of the Sea, produced by Jean-Michel Cousteau and Mose Richards. 1992. Turner Home Entertainment. Come face-to-face with the great white shark and scientists who are trying to learn more about it. Includes footage of Rodney Fox describing his terrifying attack by a great white.

Hunt for the Great White Shark, produced by Brent Mills. 1994. National Geographic Video. Join the search for great white sharks.

Sharks, produced by Nicolas Noxon. 1985. National Geographic Video. Contains scenes of a variety of shark species and an interview with marine biologist Dr. Eugenie Clark.

Sharks on Their Best Behavior, produced by Michael deGruy and Mimi Armstrong. 1991. BBC and National Geographic for Hawaii Public Television. See tiger sharks in their annual summer migration to remote islands to feed on albatross chicks.

SHARKS ON THE INTERNET

Attention, Internet surfers! You can find information about sharks by visiting the following sites:

International Shark Attack File
(See above.)
http://www.flmnh.ufl.edu/natsci/ichthyology/ichthyology.htm#top

Natal Shark Board
http://goofy.iafrica.com/~carch/

Yahoo's Biology Site *You can find a list of Internet home pages about many different kinds of sharks, as well as divers and institutions that study sharks, at:*
http://www.yahoo.com/science/biology/marine biology/sharks

THE PLACE FOR INFO ON SHARK ATTACKS

The International Shark Attack File keeps the most accurate and up-to-date information on shark attacks worldwide. You can get descriptive information about the Shark Attack File, how sharks attack, and how many fatal and nonfatal attacks have occurred over the past five years by writing to the following address:

The International Shark Attack File
Florida Museum of Natural History,
University of Florida, Gainesville, FL 32611
Phone: (904) 392-1721 FAX: (904) 392-8783

To See Sharks Swimming in the Wild

Hydrosphere, located in Pacific Palisades, California, is the only educational enterprise offering divers and nondivers (including children) the chance to view sharks in their natural habitat from inside the safety of a shark cage. These dives take place off Southern California's Channel Islands. Field trips for classes can be arranged. For information about shark-watching tours, write or call:

Hydrosphere
860 Via de la Paz Suite D3, Pacific Palisades, CA 90272
Phone: (310) 230-3334 FAX: (310) 230-3336

Adopt-a-Shark

For $25, you or your class can adopt a blue or mako shark. Of course, this doesn't mean that you will get a real, live shark delivered to your home, but you *will* receive a certificate and information about your shark. You will also receive a photograph of your species of shark. Your money will help to support shark research and education. For more information and an application, contact:

Southern California Marine Institute
820 South Seaside Avenue, Terminal Island, CA 90731
Phone: (310) 519-3172 FAX: (310) 519-1054

Southern California Marine Institute (SCMI) is a nonprofit consortium of ten universities whose purpose is to advance education and research on the marine environment. SCMI presents educational programs on sharks for all grade levels.

Whale Shark Adoption Program

For $10, you or your class can adopt a whale shark for a year. You will receive a fact sheet on whale sharks and an "adoption certificate" describing your shark and when, where, and by whom it was tagged. If the tagged shark is resighted, you will be notified where and when the resighting occurred. For more information, contact:

Shark Research Institute
P.O. Box 40, Princeton, NJ 08540
Phone: (609) 921-3522 FAX: (609) 921-1505

To See Sharks in Captivity

The following aquariums have sharks in their live exhibits:

California
Marine World Africa USA
Marine World Parkway
Vallejo, CA 94589
Phone: (707) 644-4000

Sea World of California
1720 S. Shores Drive
San Diego, CA 92109-7995
Phone: (619) 222-6363

Steinhart Aquarium
Golden Gate Park
San Francisco, CA 94118-4599
Phone: (415) 750-7295

Canada
Vancouver Aquarium
Box 3232
Vancouver, BC
Vancouver, Canada V6B 3X8
Phone: (604) 631-2505

Connecticut
Mystic Marinelife Aquarium
55 Coogan Blvd.
Mystic, CT 06355-1997
Phone: (860) 536-9631

Florida
Sea World of Florida
7007 Sea World Drive
Orlando, FL 32821-8097
Phone: (407) 363-2284

Hawaii
Sea Life Park Hawaii
Makapuu Point
Waimanalo, HI 96795-1897
Phone: (808) 259-7933

Waikiki Aquarium
2777 Kalakaua Ave.
Honolulu, HI 96815
Phone: (808) 923-9741

Illinois
Shedd Aquarium
1200 S. Lake Shore Drive
Chicago, IL 60605
Phone: (312) 939-2426

Louisiana
Aquarium of the Americas
  (Audubon)
P.O. Box 4327
New Orleans, LA 70718-4327
Phone: (504) 861-2537

Maryland

National Aquarium in Baltimore
Pier 3
501 E. Pratt St.
Baltimore, MD 21202-3194
Phone: (410) 576-3823

Massachusetts

New England Aquarium
Central Wharf
Boston, MA 02110
Phone: (617) 973-3823

New Jersey

New Jersey State Aquarium
1 Riverside Drive
Camden, NJ 08103
Phone: (609) 365-3300

New York

Aquarium for Wildlife
   Conservation
West 8th & Surf Avenue
Brooklyn, NY 11224
Phone: (718) 265-3426

North Carolina

North Carolina Aquarium
   at Fort Fisher
2201 Ft. Fisher Boulevard South
Kure Beach, NC 28449-0130
Phone: (910) 458-8259

North Carolina Aquarium
   at Pine Knoll Shores
Box 580
Atlantic Beach, NC 28512-0580
Phone: (919) 247-4004

North Carolina Aquarium
   on Roanoke Island
Box 967, Airport Road
Manteo, NC 27954
Phone: (919) 473-3494

Ohio

Sea World of Ohio
1100 Sea World Drive
Aurora, OH 44202
Phone: (216) 562-8101

Tennessee

Tennessee Aquarium
Box 11048
Chattanooga, TN 37401
Phone: (615) 266-3467

Texas

Dallas Aquarium
Box 150113
Dallas, TX 75315
Phone: (214) 670-8453

Sea World of Texas
10500 Sea World Drive
San Antonio, TX 78251
Phone: (512) 523-3635

Washington

Seattle Aquarium
Pier 59, Waterfront Park
Seattle, WA 98101-2059
Phone: (206) 386-4300

Index